To Tom and Kathy who are never bored. (Well hardly ever!)

Published by The Trumpet Club, 666 Fifth Avenue, New York, New York 10103
Copyright © 1978 by Peter Spier

ISBN: 0-440-84319-7

This edition published by arrangement with Doubleday, a division of Bantam Doubleday Dell Publishing Group, Inc. Printed in the United States of America
January 1991   UPC   10 9 8 7 6 5 4 3 2 1

BORED–NOTHING TO DO!

by Peter Spier

A TRUMPET CLUB SPECIAL EDITION

"Go do something. I was never bored at your age!"

"Let's make something."　　**"What?"**

But how?

So that's how it works.

They need wheels…and wood…and seats…and nails…

and paint... and glue... and cloth... and hinges... and rope...

and windshields...and screws...

You need a lot of stuff to build an airplane.

Hard work!

"Need wire."   **That is easy.**

How about that?

A plane needs an engine.

Too small.

Too heavy.

Just right!

Messy job. Tiring.

"To make it run, turn the key."

Noisy!...Scary!...But it works.

It flies...

It really flies.

Great plane!

TV doesn't work.
Call a repair man.

Phone doesn't work.
Go get a repair man,
and the telephone company.

Car will not start.   **(Of course not!)**

"Where are my sheets?"

"Look at the baby carriage...

and what happened to the bicycles?"

"What happened to our fence?"

"...and to my clothesline?"   "...and to the garden furniture?"

"Nothing works!" (Small wonder!)
"Where is everything?" "Where are the boys?"

"Come down immediately!!"

"I think they are angry."   "May as well go down."

Nice landing.

A good spanking (and a kiss).

"Put it all back where it belongs!"

The engine.

The gas tank.

The windows.

The chairs.

The sheets (a little bit torn).

The rope.

The paint...but how?

The wire.

The wheels.

The fence.

The wood.

The tools.

Everything.

Sent to their room. Early!

"Some boys." "Clever, too!"

Bored—nothing to do!